Dear Damion,

I hope you love this book!

We love you very much!!

Love,
Aunt Cindy
Uncle & Steve

THE
Spider
Who Saved
Christmas
A LEGEND

RAYMOND ARROYO

ILLUSTRATED BY RANDY GALLEGOS

SOPHIA
INSTITUTE PRESS

Text Copyright © 2020 by Raymond Arroyo
Images Copyright © 2020 by Randy Gallegos

Printed in Canada.

Sophia Institute Press®
Box 5284, Manchester, NH 03108
1-800-888-9344

www.SophiaInstitute.com
Sophia Institute Press· is a registered trademark of Sophia Institute.

ISBN: 978-1-64413-211-1

Library of Congress Control Number:
2020944343

FOR REBECCA

and all the mothers who spin
webs of love and sacrifice that
hold our families together.

In the days of Herod, the king of Judea, Mary, her husband, Joseph, and the Baby Jesus fled Bethlehem by night, bound for the land of Egypt.

Weary from their journey, they sought refuge in the caverns of the hill country...

And as they entered a cave, behold, a great spider trembled at the Child's cry. The sound vibrated through her golden web, filling Nephila with wonder.

She scampered to the corner of
the silk, where a sac of eggs—her
future—hung. They were safe,
swaddled in the golden strands
she had spent hours knitting
about them. She peered down at
the fascinating strangers below.

The woman, cradling the Babe
in her mantle, reclined beneath
Nephila's silken canopy.

The man with kind eyes lifted
his lantern, staring into the
darkness outside the cave.

"We can't stay here, Mary,"
he said in a soft voice.
"Herod's men are coming."

For he had been warned in
a dream that King Herod
sought to destroy the Child.

"Jesus won't be safe until we reach Egypt."

Mary nodded gently,
kissing the head of her Babe.

"Fear not, Joseph."

Nephila dropped on a line of webbing to get a closer look at
the Child, who seemed to glow with His own radiance.

Joseph's eyes turned hard when he spotted the dangling
visitor above Mary. "Be still. There are spiders," he spat out.

He slashed at Nephila with his staff.
As she recoiled, Joseph ran his staff though the web,
ripping two of the main lines.

The golden-backed spider retreated
into the shadows and laid her body
protectively over her sac of children.

"Leave it, Joseph,"
Mary said.

"They are dangerous."

He lifted the lantern, seeking
the spider lurking in the
dark. As he raised his
staff to strike the spider
and clear what was left
of the webbing, Mary
took hold of the rod.

"All are here for a
reason. Let it be."

ow, at the hum of the woman's voice, Nephila relaxed but dared not leave the shadows. She rubbed her two front legs together, wondering how she would ever repair the shredded web.

"Rest, Joseph." Mary patted the ground beside her.

Joseph lay next to the Child and threw his cloak over the three of them.

And behold, wails of anguish
and the final cries of babies
floated through the night.

Nephila stiffened at the sound of the wails on the wind.

"Poor children," Joseph said. "The soldiers are close."

"Dim the light," Mary whispered.

"I am sorry we are in this horrible place," he told her,
snuffing out the lantern light. "We are so exposed."

"It is where we are meant to be. There is beauty, even here." She
looked up at Nephila's web, touching Joseph's hand. "And love."

"Pray for our safety," he said, closing his eyes.
Mary lightly moved her lips. Only the faraway
shrieks disturbed the cave's silence.

Nephila moved to the tattered edge of her silk. Taking advantage of the stillness, she began to spin a new web. How would she ever reattach the ripped drape to the faraway wall? It would take hours — days perhaps.

A shaft a moonlight suddenly
cut into the cave.

As Nephila turned toward the light,
a warm gust carrying the sweet
scent of berries blew over her.

It swirled about the cavern, and
she felt herself rising slightly.

The wispy main lines of her web floated
up to the ceiling and stretched to the
far wall of the cave as if they had never
been disturbed. The spider warily walked
the length of the silk to the far cave wall,
testing the strength of the new lines.

Suddenly, the Child below cried, sending a vibration through the web. Nephila's egg sac leapt and rippled at the sound.

The spider stared down at the Child — this Jesus.

Never had she felt such a sensation. She instantly understood what she had to do.

At the center of her web, she plucked the strings, playing a tune only spiders could hear. From deep within the crevice of the cave, Nephila's older children scuttled forward by the dozens. Each heard its mother's call and followed her to the cave opening.

Nephila hung upside down from the
cave's mouth and descended on a thick
golden line until she reached the floor.

She then climbed to the corners of the opening
and repeatedly fluttered across the center line,
leaving a trail of golden thread behind her.

Her framework completed, she plucked on the center strand. At the sound, her children sprang into action, dropping cords of web, weaving their golden silk in a frantic, rhythmic dance.

ow when it was daybreak, and
the spiders' work was done,
the cave mouth wore a golden veil of
webbing—sealing it completely.

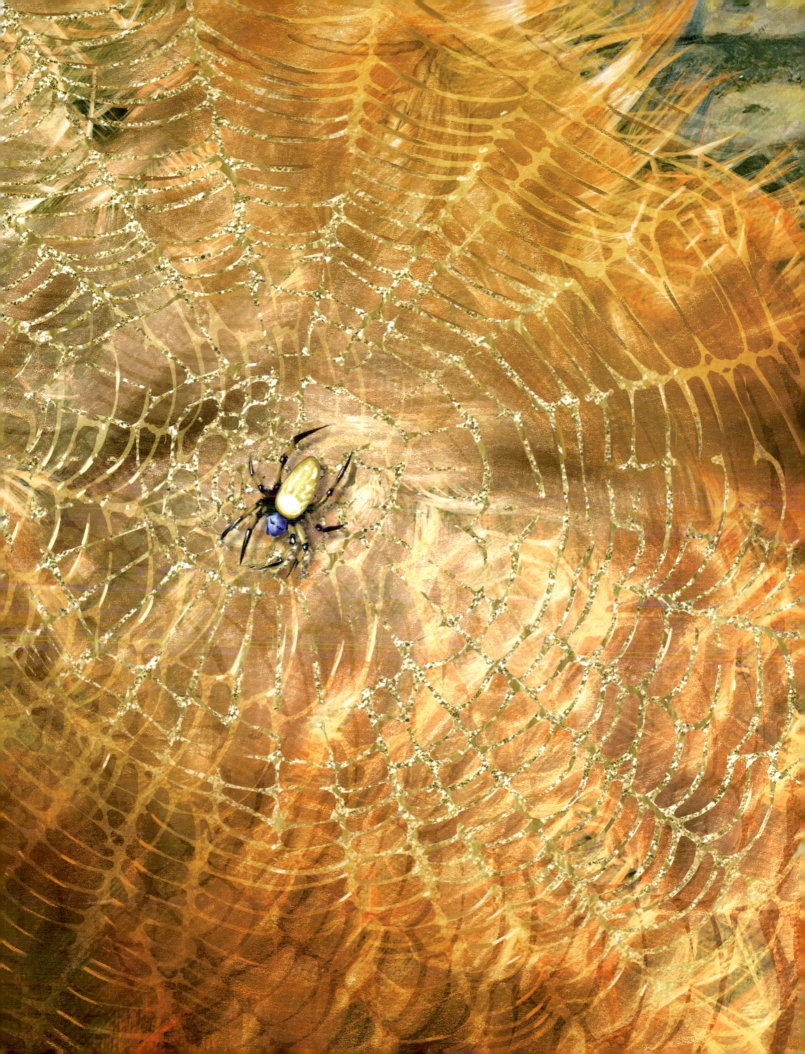

Nephila's children returned to the
darkness and their personal webs.

But not Nephila.

Despite the frost dotting the golden
curtain, she rested on the outside,
at the very center of the web.

And it came to pass that Nephila felt the approach of three soldiers climbing the hillside. They carried blood-slicked swords and spoke in loud, crude voices.

"You two get up there and inspect the cave," one soldier yelled.

"Why would a baby boy be in a cave?"

"You have your orders! Inspect every dwelling and kill every boy under two — especially the newborns. That was Herod's command. Go!"

A pair of soldiers clambered up to the cave.

The yelling and clanging of
armor woke Joseph, though
Mary and Jesus did not stir.

In silence, Joseph fetched
his staff and held it high,
ready to defend his family.

The golden screen blocking the
outside world puzzled him.

On its thick gauze he observed
the shadows of two huge
soldiers, one waving a sword.

Joseph tightened his grip on the staff.

Outside, the sunlight caused the frosted cobweb to glimmer and sparkle. Nephila wished to return to the shadowy recesses of the cave. She felt so exposed sitting in the daylight. But the Child had clearly told her to spin a web over the entranceway and remain there.

"What should we do?" one of the soldiers whispered, considering the spiders' handiwork. "No one entered this cave, or the web would be broken."

"You are right." The soldier glared at Nephila, whose legs were pulsing. "There is no newborn in there—except maybe newborn spiders!"

"That thing looks ready to pounce," the other soldier said, shivering for an instant. "I hate spiders. Forget it. Let's go."

"Everything is clear up here, commander," one of them yelled. And they retreated, running down the hill.

Inside the cave, Joseph lowered his staff and fell against the rocky wall, giving thanks for their safety.

Nephila watched the soldiers leave. And after a long while, she began to bow on the strings of her web.

The light melody awakened Mary.

"Joseph, from where is that music coming?"

"I hear nothing," he said.

Mary marveled at the gossamer gauze and the shadow of Nephila, illuminated by the sun.

"Isn't it beautiful?"

"Soldiers came as you slept.
The spider saved Jesus, and us,"
Joseph said, staring at the web.

"Yes? All are here for a reason." Mary looked
lovingly at her Son and nodded off to sleep.

esus, Mary, and Joseph
remained in the cave another
day before taking their leave.

They pulled back a piece of Nephila's
golden curtain to pass from the
cave, and the Child's hand grazed
the web as they hastened to Egypt.

And it came to pass that Nephila withdrew to the
cave, where she tenderly embraced her egg sac
until the last of her spiderlings came forth.

Soon after, she repaired the golden curtain
at the entryway and spent her days at
its center. Basking in the sunlight, she
awaited the return of the Child with
the sweet cry she could never forget.

Even today, Golden Silk Orb Weavers, the
children of Nephila, can be found on
their webs, in the sun, waiting, waiting...

And theirs is considered the most
precious of all spiders' silk.

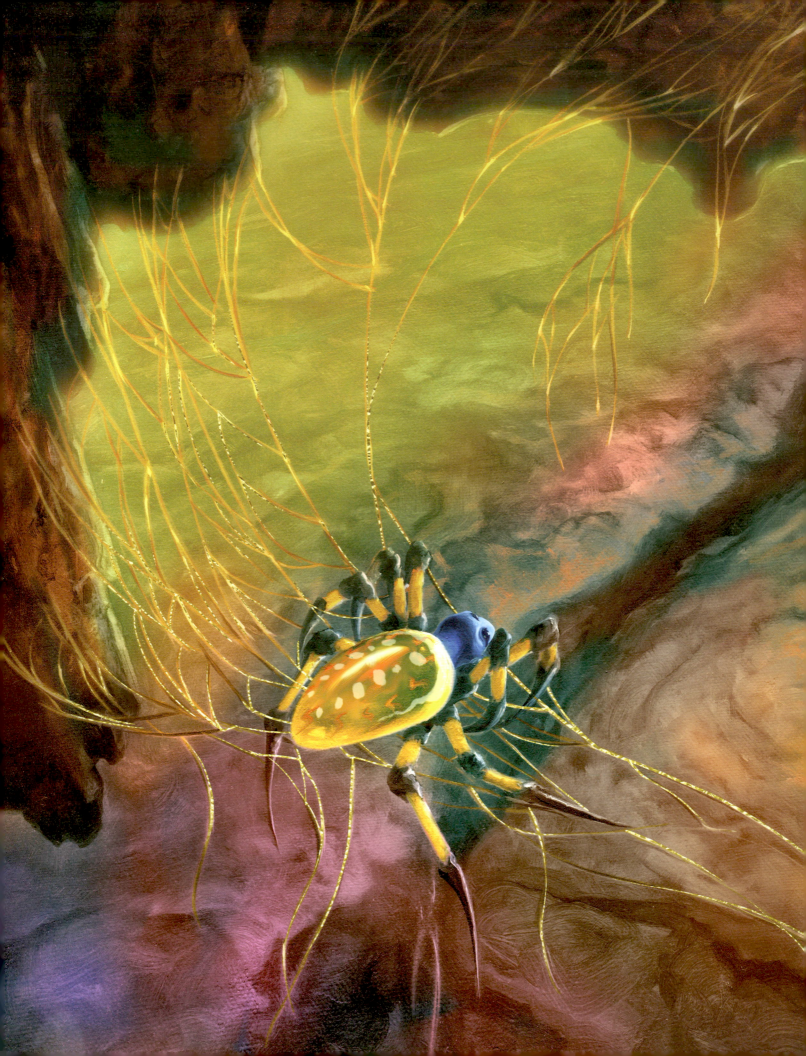

ephila's gift to the Christ Child is remembered in the sparkling tinsel that drips from evergreens all over the world at Christmastime.

Poles, Ukrainians, and other Eastern Europeans have a tradition of placing spider ornaments on Christmas trees to commemorate the spider that saved Christmas.

So next time you see some twinkling tinsel or a spider ornament lurking in a tree branch, think of Nephila, who, though small and feared, met divinity and reflected His light as only she could.

Like each of us...

She was there for a reason.

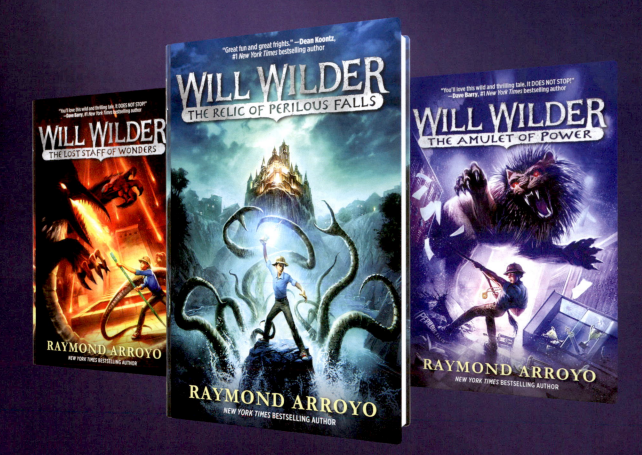